Emmy Payne

Katy
No-Pocket

Pictures by H. A. Rey

Houghton Mifflin Company, Boston

Big tears rolled down Katy Kangaroo's brown face. Poor Katy was crying because she didn't have a pocket like other mother kangaroos. Freddy was Katy Kangaroo's little boy and he needed a pocket to ride in. All grown-up kangaroos take awfully big hops and little kangaroos, like Freddy, get left far behind unless their mothers have nice pockets to carry them in.

And poor Katy didn't have any pocket at all.

Katy Kangaroo cried just thinking about it, and Freddy cried, too.

Then, all of a sudden, Katy had a wonderful idea! It was so wonderful she jumped six feet up in the air.

The idea was this. Other animal mothers had children and they didn't have any pockets. She'd go and ask one of them how they carried their babies!

Freddy looked all around to see whom to ask and Katy looked all around to see, too. And what they both saw were two bubbles rising up from the river right beside them.

"Mrs. Crocodile!" said Katy, feeling lots better already. "*She* hasn't any pocket. Let's ask her!"

A lot of big muddy bubbles came up through the water and

then Mrs. Crocodile stuck her head up and opened her *enormous* mouth and smiled.

"Why, Katy Kangaroo! What can I do for you today?"

"Please, Mrs. Crocodile, I am so sad," said Katy. "I have no pocket and Freddy has to walk wherever we go and he gets so tired. Oh dear, oh dear!"

And she started to cry again.

The crocodile began to cry, too, and then she said, "B-b–but — What — what can *I* do?"

"You can tell me how to carry Freddy," said Katy. "How do you carry little Catherine Crocodile? Oh, do *please* tell me."

"Why, I carry her on my back, of course!" said Mrs. Crocodile.

She was so surprised that anyone shouldn't know that she forgot to cry any more.

hy on my back, of course!

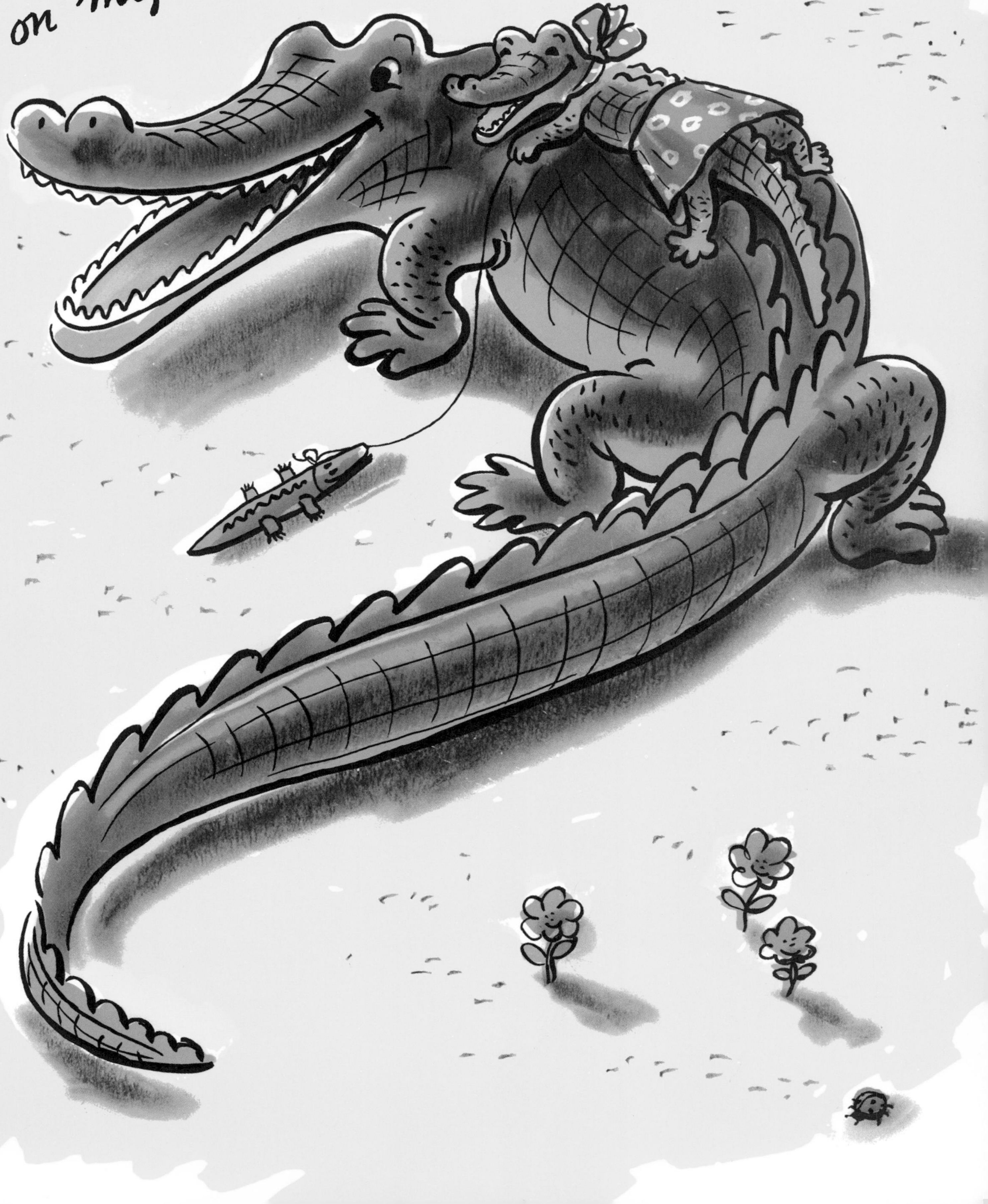

Katy was pleased. She said, "Thank you," and as soon as she got to a good squatting-down place, she squatted and said, "Now, Freddy, climb on my back. After this it will be so simple — no trouble at all."

But it wasn't simple. In the first place, Freddy could not crawl up onto her back because his knees stuck out. He couldn't hang on because his front legs were too short. And when he did manage to hang on for a few minutes and Katy gave a long hop, he fell off — bump, bang — with a terrific thump.

So Katy saw that she couldn't carry her baby on her back.

Katy and Freddy sat down again and thought and thought.
"I know! I'll ask Mrs. Monkey. I'm sure she can help
me."

So Katy and Freddy set off for the forest and very soon
they found Mrs. Monkey. She had her young son, Jocko,
with her and Katy Kangaroo hurried so to catch up with
them that she was almost out of breath. But, finally, she
managed to squeak, "Please, Mrs. Monkey, how do you
carry Jocko?"

"Why, in my arms, of course," said Mrs. Monkey. "How
else would any sensible animal carry anything?" And she
whisked away through the trees.

"Oh dear," said Katy, and a great
big tear ran across her long nose.
"I can't carry anything in
these short little arms,
oh *dear!* She wasn't
any help at all. What
are we going to do?"
And she just sat down
and cried harder than
ever.

Poor Freddy! He hated to see his mother cry, so he put his paw to his head and he thought, and thought, and *thought*.

"What about the lion?" he asked when Katy stopped crying a little.

"They don't carry their children. The poor things walk just the way you do," said Katy.

the way the Lions do it

the way the Birds do it

"There's — there's birds,"
said Freddy. "How do
they carry their babies?"

"Birds!" said Katy. "The mother birds push their children
out of the nest and they squawk and shriek and flap their
wings about it."

Then all at once Katy Kangaroo stopped crying and looked at Freddy. "They do say that the owl knows almost everything," she said slowly.

"Well, then, for goodness' sake, let's ask *him!*" said
Freddy. They found the owl asleep in an old dead tree,

and he was cross because he didn't want to be waked up in the middle of the day. But when he saw that Katy was so sad he came out, blinking and ruffling his feathers and said in a scratchy voice, "Well! Well! what is it? Speak up! And speak loudly. I'm deaf as a post."

So Katy stood under the tree and screamed at him, "I'm a mother kangaroo and I haven't a pocket to carry my child in. How shall I carry him? What shall I do?"

"Get a pocket," said the owl and went to sleep again.

"Where?" cried Katy. "Oh, please, don't go to sleep before you tell me where!"

"How should I know?" said the owl. "They sell that sort of thing in the City, I believe. Now, kindly go away and let me sleep."

"The City!" said Katy, and looked at Freddy with big, round eyes. "Of course, we'll go to the City!"

Katy was so excited that
she almost left Freddy behind as she went leaping over
bushes and hopping along the path, singing in a sort of

hummy way a little song she had just made up:

"Hippity! Hoppity!
Flippity! Floppity!
Wasn't it a pity?
I didn't know
It was to the City
I should go!"

She hopped so fast that Freddy could hardly keep up, but at last they left the woods behind and came to the City

where there were stores and houses and automobiles.

The people all stared and stared at Katy, but she didn't notice it. She was looking for pockets and she saw that almost everybody had them.

And then, all at once, she saw — she could hardly believe it — a man who seemed to be ALL pockets! He was simply covered with pockets. Big pockets, little pockets, medium-sized pockets —

Katy went up to him and laid a paw on his arm. He was a little frightened, but Katy looked at him with her soft brown eyes and said, "Please, dear, kind man, where did you get all those pockets?"

"These pockets?" he said. "You want to know where I got all these pockets? Why, they just came with the apron, of course."

"You mean you can really get something to put on with ALL those pockets already in it?" asked Katy.

"Sure you can," said the man. "I keep my hammer and nails and tools in my pockets, but I can get another apron, so I'll give you mine."

He took off the apron

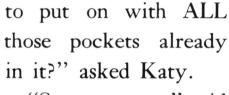

and dumped it

UPSIDE DOWN.

Out fell a saw, wrench, nails, a hammer, a drill, and lots of other tools. Then the man shook the apron hard and turned it right side up again and hung it around Katy's neck and tied it behind her back.

Katy was so pleased and excited and happy that she couldn't speak. She just stood still and looked down at the pockets and smiled and smiled and smiled.

By this time, a big crowd had gathered to see what Katy Kangaroo was doing. When they saw how pleased she was, they all smiled, too.

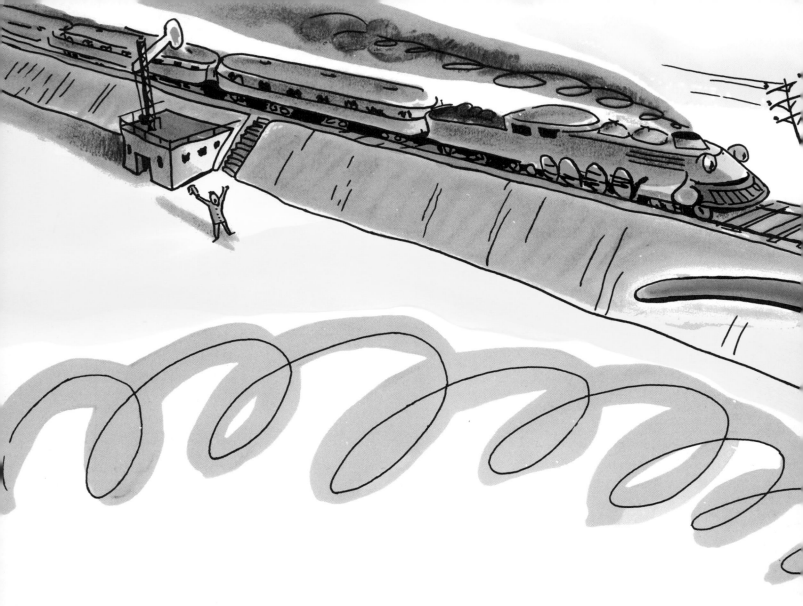

At last Katy was able to say "Thank you" to the nice, kind man, and then what do you think she did? She popped Freddy into a very comfortable pocket and she hippity-hopped home faster than ever before because, of course, she didn't have to wait for Freddy.

And when she got home, what do you think she did?

Well, she had so many pockets that she put Freddy into the biggest one of all. Then, into the next largest she put little Leonard Lion. Thomas Tortoise just fitted into another pocket.

Sometimes she had a baby bird if its mother was busy at a worm hunt. And there was still room for a monkey, a skunk, a rabbit, a raccoon, a lizard, a squirrel, a 'possum, a turtle, a frog, and a snail.

So now, all the animals
like Katy's pockets better than
any other pockets in the whole forest.

And Katy Kangaroo
is very happy because now
SHE HAS MORE POCKETS THAN
ANY MOTHER KANGAROO
IN THE WORLD!

The End